④ Camera team and studio staff in action

⑤ Sports coverage from a mobile unit

⑥ Lighting gantry for a studio set

What appears on a television screen is something familiar to millions. What happens before such an image appears is a mystery to most people.

This book explains the intricate and complex nature of television from the television camera, through sound and vision control, studios and outside broadcasts, to eventual transmission and reception.

Acknowledgment:
The publishers gratefully acknowledge the assistance of the following in the preparation of this book:
AKG Acoustics Ltd; Pye TVT Limited; Autocue Products Ltd; Oxford Scientific Films Ltd; IBA Engineering Information Service; Engineering Information Department, BBC; S R Ellerker, of Ingram, Phillips and Austen, Optometrists; Rank Cintel; Mullard Ltd;
In particular, the publishers would like to place on record their appreciation of the whole-hearted co-operation of the staff of Yorkshire Television, without which the production of this book would have been impossible.

Revised edition

HOW IT WORKS . . .
TELEVISION

by R P A EDWARDS
Technical Consultant
J Q ROGERS B Eng, C Eng, MIEE
Chief Engineer, Yorkshire Television
illustrated by GERALD WITCOMB MSIAD

Ladybird Books Loughborough

Introduction

As you watch a television programme, vision and sound are reaching your receiver by means of radio waves travelling at the speed of light. In the television studio, cameras convert light into electric currents and microphones do the same with sound. These currents are amplified, converted to electromagnetic waves and transmitted through an aerial. They pass through the atmosphere to the aerial of your receiver. In the receiver they are changed back to electric currents which are used to recreate vision and sound. This book explains how these processes are carried out.

Colour and light

To understand how colour television works one must

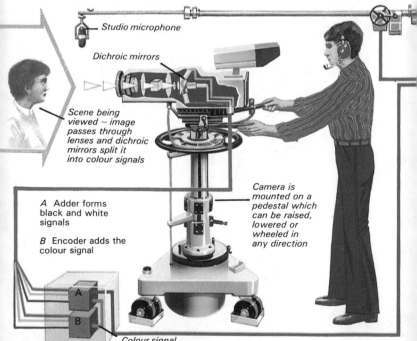

Studio microphone

Dichroic mirrors

Scene being viewed – image passes through lenses and dichroic mirrors split it into colour signals

A Adder forms black and white signals

B Encoder adds the colour signal

Camera is mounted on a pedestal which can be raised, lowered or wheeled in any direction

Colour signal

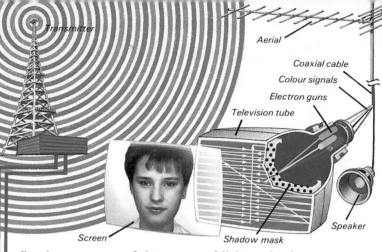

Transmitter

Aerial

Coaxial cable

Colour signals

Electron guns

Television tube

Screen

Shadow mask

Speaker

first have a grasp of the nature of light and colour. Light travels in the form of waves at 300 000 kilometres per second (186 000 miles per second). White light is actually a combination of several colours. If you shine light through a prism onto a white surface it will produce a rainbow-like band of colours called a spectrum. All the colours of the spectrum are combinations of any two of the primary colours, red, green and blue.

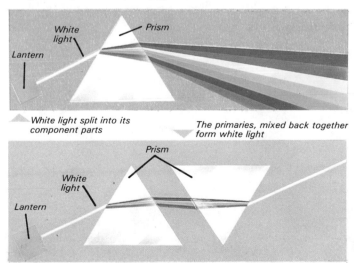

Lantern

White light

Prism

White light split into its component parts

The primaries, mixed back together form white light

Prism

White light

Lantern

5

Each colour has a different wavelength, which is the distance between the peaks of the waves. We can also measure waves by their frequency, which is the number of cycles which pass a given point in a second.

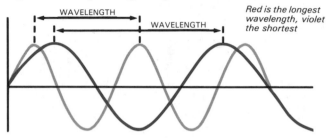

WAVELENGTH

WAVELENGTH

Red is the longest wavelength, violet the shortest

Light has extremely short wavelengths with violet being the shortest at about 400 nanometres. A nanometre is a 1 000 000 000th of a metre. Red has the longest wavelength at around 700 nanometres. We see colours because of the way our eyes respond to these waves.

Spectral colours should not be confused with those of paints and dyes, which we call artists' colours. Spectral colours are additive while artists' colours are subtractive.

Additive colours

By combining any two spectral primaries we produce a

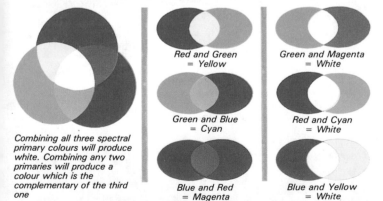

Combining all three spectral primary colours will produce white. Combining any two primaries will produce a colour which is the complementary of the third one

Red and Green = Yellow

Green and Blue = Cyan

Blue and Red = Magenta

Green and Magenta = White

Red and Cyan = White

Blue and Yellow = White

colour which is the opposite or complementary of the third spectral primary.

You can prove that yellow light contains only red and green wavelengths by trying the experiment shown below. Cyan, a light blue, is a mixture of green and blue light and also appears in the spectrum. Magenta (red and blue wavelengths) does not appear in the spectrum or in nature. It is said to be a non-spectral colour and is in fact white with the green wavelengths removed.

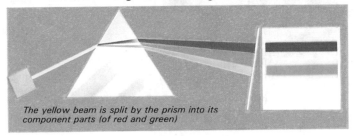

The yellow beam is split by the prism into its component parts (of red and green)

Subtractive colours

The primaries of artists' colours are red, blue and yellow. Shine a white light through a prism onto a yellow surface. You will see that one colour of the spectrum is missing. The yellow has absorbed or subtracted it.

Repeat the experiment with surfaces of the other two primary colours and see which colours are subtracted.

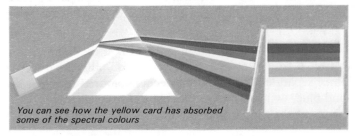

You can see how the yellow card has absorbed some of the spectral colours

The colour television camera

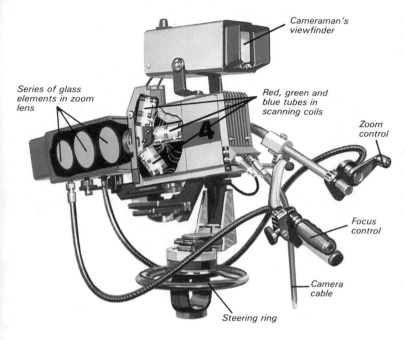

Cameraman's viewfinder

Series of glass elements in zoom lens

Red, green and blue tubes in scanning coils

Zoom control

Focus control

Camera cable

Steering ring

A prism has an important role in a colour television camera. The prism used is much more complicated than the one used in your experiments. Instead of emitting the light in the form of a spectrum, it gives out separate rays of red, green and blue as you can see in the illustration on page 47.

The colour-splitting prism system takes the light reflected from the scene being televised and splits it into three separate versions of the scene, coloured red, green and blue, which are then focused onto the glass face plates of the three camera tubes.

The camera tube

When light enters the face plate of the tube it passes through the transparent tin-oxide layer and strikes the photoconductive layer. Light makes this a conductor of electricity; the more light it receives, the better it conducts. In effect, the light from the object being televised builds up an image on the photoconductive layer made up of areas of varying conductivity.

At the other end of the tube the cathode of an electron gun emits a stream of electrons. These are directed by focusing and deflection coils so that the electrons scan the whole of the image from left to right, line by line, from top left to the bottom right-hand corner.

As the electron beam strikes a point on the photoconductive layer it completes a circuit between it and the conductive layer behind and a flow of electric current takes place. The brighter the point on the image, the stronger the flow. The electric current is the picture or video signal.

THE CAMERA TUBE

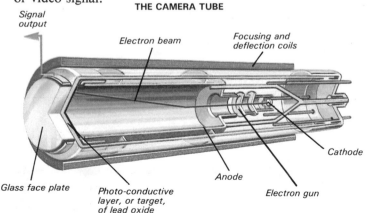

Signal output

Electron beam

Focusing and deflection coils

Cathode

Glass face plate

Photo-conductive layer, or target, of lead oxide

Anode

Electron gun

More about scanning

The scanning beam moves extremely fast. In the system used in Europe the beam moves across the target 625 times to scan each picture. For this reason it is known as the 625 line system.

The picture in the form of the image on the target is scanned twenty-five times per second, in two passes.

During the first pass, known as the first field, the beam scans 312½ lines, flying back to the left side after each line. At the end of the pass it flies back to the top to start the scan of the next 312½ lines in between those of the first scan. This is called *interlace*.

Each scan of 312½ lines is a field, whereas the complete 625 lines is a picture. This technique reduces flicker.

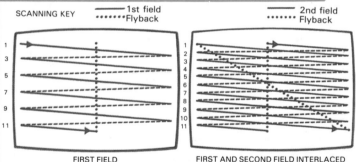

Television pictures are made up of hundreds of horizontal lines, known as interlaced scanning. An electron beam first scans all the odd numbered lines, then all the even numbered lines (the illustrations show only a few of the 625 lines)

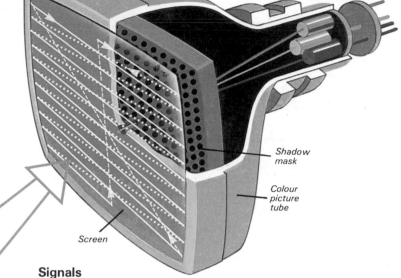

Shadow
mask

Colour
picture
tube

Screen

Signals

All three camera tubes will have been scanning in
synchronism and the current from each tube will have
passed through the camera's amplifiers to make the signals
larger. The next step is to combine these three signals
into a single signal suitable for transmission or recording.

Because many people still have monochrome receivers,
the signal has to be in a form that can be used by either
monochrome or colour receivers. Such a signal is called
compatible.

A monochrome receiver does not need the colour
information, since the picture on its screen consists of
degrees of brightness ranging from black to white. There
are still monochrome broadcasts on occasions, when an
old black and white film is transmitted.

Compatibility is obtained by transmitting separate
signals for brightness and colour. The *luminance* signal
indicates the level of brightness and the *chrominance* or
colouring signal contains the colour information.

11

The luminance signal

One way of generating the luminance (brightness) signal would be to have a fourth tube in the camera. However, since white light is a mixture of the primary colours, part of the output of the red, green and blue tubes may be combined in the following fixed proportions: Red – 30%, Green – 60%, Blue – 10%, to make the luminance signal.

The colouring signals

To enable the original red, green and blue signals to be recovered in your receiver, three signals have to be transmitted. Since the luminance signal is made up of fixed parts of the three colour signals, two further signals called colour difference signals are transmitted. They are *red minus luminance* and *blue minus luminance*.

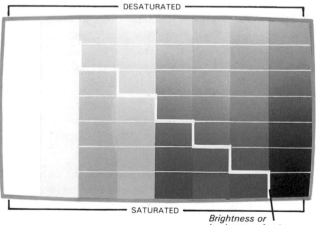

DESATURATED

SATURATED

Brightness or luminance of colour

The chrominance signal

The colour difference signals are combined into a chrominance signal and added to the luminance signal (brightness) before recording or transmission.

More about colour encoding

Three items of information have to be contained in the video (vision) signal: brightness, colour, known as hue, and the depth of colour, known as saturation. Brightness is provided by the luminance signal so the chrominance signals have to provide information about hue (colour) and saturation. By saturation is meant how deep is the colour (hue). A pale hue is one which is very diluted with white light. So in television, a very deep colour is termed saturated and a pale one desaturated.

So information about brightness is contained in the luminance signal, hue and saturation in the chrominance signal. It is the amount of energy or *amplitude* of the colour difference signals which indicates the degree of saturation.

The red and blue signals from the camera cannot be transmitted as they are, as they would interfere with each other and with the luminance signal. To avoid this they are used to modulate or change the amplitude of a carrier signal. One carrier is used for each colour difference signal.

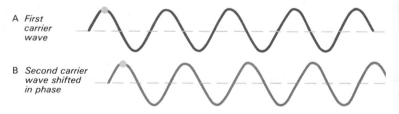

A *First carrier wave*

B *Second carrier wave shifted in phase*

These carrier waves, or subcarriers as they are called, are of the same frequency. To prevent them interfering with each other they are shifted in phase, or position, so that the peak of one wave occurs when the other is passing through zero.

These modulated subcarrier waves are now combined and are not separated until they arrive at your receiver.

Synchronisation

In television systems it is necessary for the scanning electron beam in the gun to be in the same position in the receiver as it is in the camera at any point in time. At the end of each line of scan there is a very brief blank period of a few microseconds (millionths of a second). This is known as the line blanking period during which time a pulse called a synchronising pulse is sent to the receiver to tell the scanning beam to fly back to be ready to start the next line. Pulses are also sent

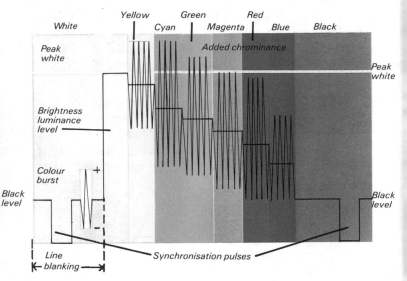

during the blank period at the end of each picture known as the field blanking period. These pulses tell the receiver circuits to return the electron beam to the top of the screen. To enable the colour information to be decoded a short burst of the colour subcarrier is also sent during this time to synchronise the receiver chrominance circuits.

Transmission
The carrier wave

The signal emitted by the camera is much too weak for transmission. In all broadcasting, both video and audio, a powerful wave of constant amplitude but much higher frequency is used as a vehicle. This is known as the carrier wave. The signal to be transmitted is combined with the carrier wave by a process known as modulation.

AMPLITUDE MODULATION

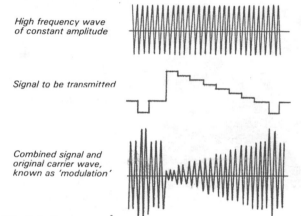

High frequency wave of constant amplitude

Signal to be transmitted

Combined signal and original carrier wave, known as 'modulation'

Modulation

There are two forms of modulation, amplitude (AM) and frequency (FM). For video signals, earth-based transmitters use AM while satellites use FM. The audio signal for television is also FM.

Amplitude modulation consists of varying the amplitude of the carrier wave in the same proportions as the signal to be transmitted.

In frequency modulation the frequency of the carrier is varied by the amplitude of the signal to be transmitted.

The transmitter network

A typical television transmitter mast

Unlike the longer wavelengths used in radio broadcasting, the ultra high frequency (UHF) waves used in television broadcasting are not very well reflected back to earth by the ionosphere. Television signals travel in straight lines like light and do not follow the curve of the earth's surface. To overcome this problem, the country is covered by a network of television transmitters with very high aerial masts. Each station receives signals by cable or microwave link and transmits them so that virtually the whole country is covered.

Transmitter equipment being tested

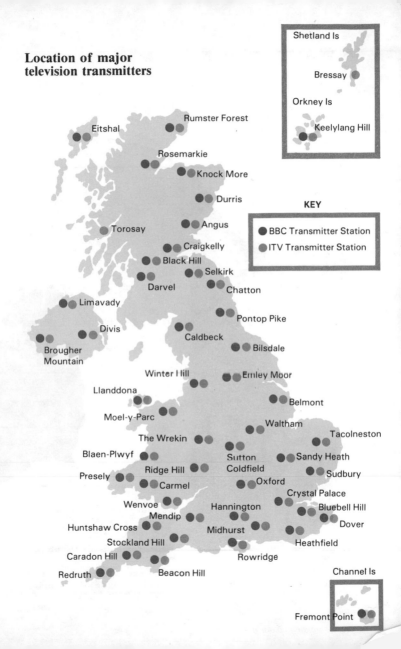

**Location of major
television transmitters**

Shetland Is

Bressay

Orkney Is

Keelylang Hill

Eitshal

Rumster Forest

Rosemarkie

Knock More

Durris

KEY

Angus

Torosay

● BBC Transmitter Station
● ITV Transmitter Station

Craigkelly

Black Hill

Selkirk

Darvel

Chatton

Limavady

Pontop Pike

Divis

Caldbeck

Brougher
Mountain

Bilsdale

Winter Hill

Emley Moor

Llanddona

Belmont

Moel-y-Parc

Waltham

The Wrekin

Tacolneston

Blaen-Plwyf

Sutton
Coldfield

Sandy Heath

Presely

Ridge Hill

Sudbury

Carmel

Oxford

Crystal Palace

Wenvoe

Hannington

Bluebell Hill

Mendip

Dover

Huntshaw Cross

Midhurst

Heathfield

Stockland Hill

Caradon Hill

Rowridge

Redruth

Beacon Hill

Channel Is

Fremont Point

The television receiver

The heart of a television receiver is the colour picture tube. The most common type is a cathode ray tube with three electron guns arranged in a triangle.

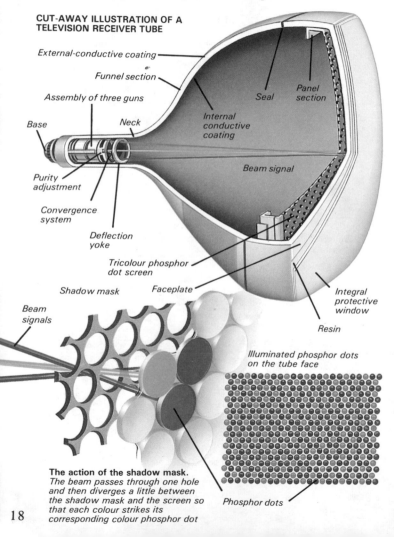

CUT-AWAY ILLUSTRATION OF A TELEVISION RECEIVER TUBE

External-conductive coating

Funnel section

Assembly of three guns

Base

Neck

Seal

Panel section

Internal conductive coating

Purity adjustment

Beam signal

Convergence system

Deflection yoke

Tricolour phosphor dot screen

Shadow mask

Faceplate

Integral protective window

Beam signals

Resin

Illuminated phosphor dots on the tube face

The action of the shadow mask.
The beam passes through one hole and then diverges a little between the shadow mask and the screen so that each colour strikes its corresponding colour phosphor dot

Phosphor dots

18

The inner surface of the tube is covered with groups of phosphor dots which glow briefly when struck by an electron beam. The dots are arranged in groups of three called triads. In each triad there is a dot which will glow blue, another red and the third, green. In a 20 inch receiver there will be 400 000 of these triads.

As in the camera, deflection coils cause the electron beams to scan the screen. Behind the screen is a metal grill called a shadow mask. The mask has as many holes as there are triads. The electron guns are so angled that the beams from all three hit the same hole simultaneously. As each beam emerges on the other side it can only hit a phosphor dot of its own colour (*see* diagram opposite).

The phosphors

Each of the triads of phosphors is known as an element. As each element is excited it will continue to glow for about 1/50th of a second. Its colour will be a blend according to the proportion of the three primary colours emitted by the element. That, of course, depends upon the amplitude of the three colour signals which are decoded within the receiver circuits.

As each element continues to glow for approximately the duration of a field scan, the effect is for the whole screen to glow continually.

A television picture of a moving subject, like that in a cinema film, is really a very rapid sequence of still pictures. Each time the picture is scanned by the cameras the actors on the set will have moved ever so slightly. With a film camera, every time a frame is photographed the actors on the film studio set will have moved a little too. As we watch the screen our eyes fill the tiny time gap between film frames or television picture scans with the 'memory' of the previous one.

The Trinitron*

There are other types of receiver, the most popular of which is the Trinitron type. This has vertical phosphor stripes arranged in threes instead of triads of dots. The shadow mask is made of vertical wires held very tautly between two bars. There is only one electron gun but it has three cathodes in a horizontal row. Since the beams only have to be made to converge on a horizontal plane convergence plates are used instead of coils. This and other differences make it a cheaper set to produce and it produces a brighter image. (*Registered Trade Mark).

DIAGRAM OF TRINITRON ELECTRON GUN ARRANGEMENT

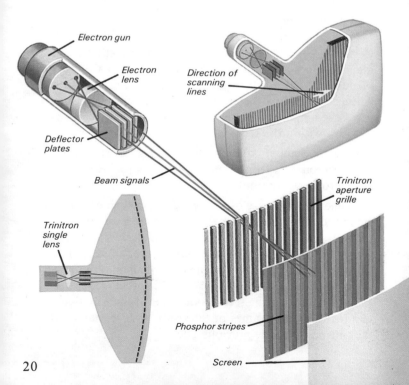

Electron gun

Electron lens

Deflector plates

Direction of scanning lines

Beam signals

Trinitron single lens

Trinitron aperture grille

Phosphor stripes

Screen

Sound

We perceive what we call 'sound' because our ears can pick up vibrations in the air for our brains to translate. These vibrations are in the form of waves but they are physical, not electromagnetic. They can only travel through air, liquids and solids. In space there is no sound. In order to convert sound waves to electromagnetic ones microphones are used.

The principle of the microphone is that vibrations in the air set up corresponding vibrations in a diaphragm. There are several types of microphone but the most commonly used in television are the capacitor and moving coil types.

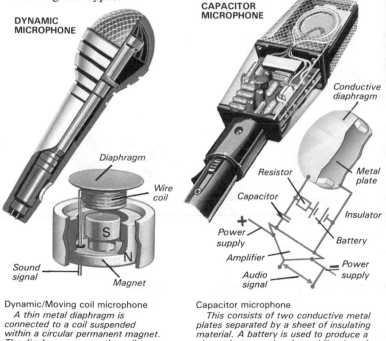

DYNAMIC MICROPHONE

CAPACITOR MICROPHONE

Diaphragm

Wire coil

Sound signal

Magnet

Conductive diaphragm

Resistor

Metal plate

Capacitor

Insulator

Power supply

Battery

Amplifier

Power supply

Audio signal

Dynamic/Moving coil microphone
A thin metal diaphragm is connected to a coil suspended within a circular permanent magnet. The diaphragm causes the coil to move within the magnet and thus sets up an electric current in the coil in sympathy with the sound.

Capacitor microphone
This consists of two conductive metal plates separated by a sheet of insulating material. A battery is used to produce a charge between the plates. Vibration of the diaphragm causes a current to flow through the resistor in sympathy with the sound.

Modulation (for diagram, *see* page 15)

As with the video signal, the sound is transmitted by modulating a carrier wave. Because of the narrow bandwidth available there is a risk that the audio signal might interfere with the video signal. To reduce this risk FM, frequency modulation, is used. This has the added advantage of providing a much better reception since FM is much less prone to interference by static, electric motors, etc., than is AM.

Telecine

This is the process by which a video signal is obtained from a film. There are two methods in use, both of which have advantages and disadvantages. They are the camera tube and the flying spot methods.

Camera tube telecine

This is the simplest method. The film is run through a projector but instead of a screen being used, lenses focus the beam directly into a television camera, usually of the plumbicon type.

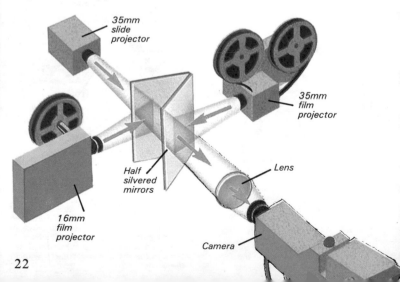

A film is made up of a number of frames each of which is a separate photograph of the scene being filmed. A film projector is used which moves 25 frames through its gate per second. The projector has a shutter resembling that in a still camera. For each frame this shutter opens twice, the first time for the camera to scan the odd-numbered field, the second for the even-numbered field scan.

Flying spot telecine

In this method a light beam from a cathode ray tube is used. A single electron gun emitting a constant beam scans a cathode ray face or screen. The moving spot of light shines through the film into lenses which pass the light through a set of colour splitting prisms. It is then collected by photoelectric cells.

The film moves continuously and during the scanning the cathode ray tube shuts off for the split second during the line and field flyback periods.

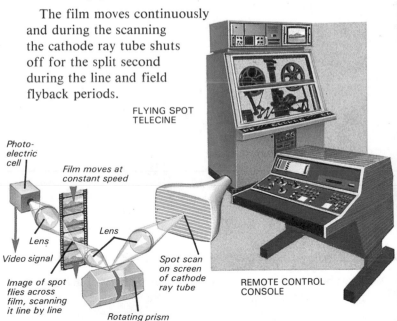

FLYING SPOT TELECINE

Photo-electric cell

Film moves at constant speed

Lens

Lens

Video signal

Spot scan on screen of cathode ray tube

Image of spot flies across film, scanning it line by line

Rotating prism

REMOTE CONTROL CONSOLE

23

Video recording

The principles in video recording are much the same as those in audio recording. Magnetic tape moves past recording heads which modulate the magnetic field as the input voltage varies. The tape speed is much higher though and the head, or heads, move on a revolving drum. There are two types of video recorder, transverse scan and helical scan. Reel-to-reel and cassette versions are available.

Transverse scan videotape recorders

In these, the tape moves horizontally, as in an audio recorder but much faster, at 400 mm per second while four heads on a drum rotating 250 times per second move vertically across the tape.

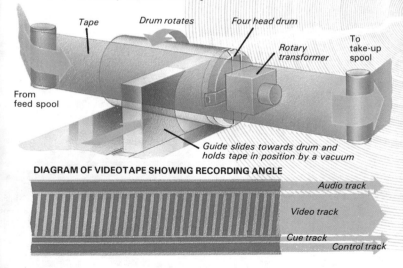

From feed spool

Tape   Drum rotates   Four head drum

Rotary transformer

To take-up spool

Guide slides towards drum and holds tape in position by a vacuum

DIAGRAM OF VIDEOTAPE SHOWING RECORDING ANGLE

Audio track

Video track

Cue track

Control track

The tape used is 50 mm wide and the recorder inscribes about 50 metres of track per second. Each of the vertical tracks will contain 18 television lines.

Helical scan videotape recorders

In this type of machine a 25 mm or 18 mm tape wraps obliquely round the head drum. The drum revolves horizontally, but because the tape is angled an oblique track results. This longer track contains a complete field

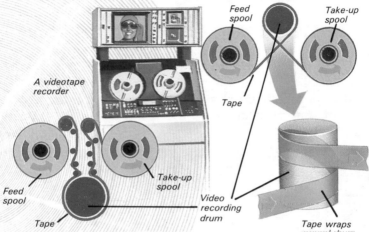

HELICAL SCAN, ALPHA WRAP FORMAT

Feed spool

Take-up spool

A videotape recorder

Tape

Feed spool

Take-up spool

Video recording drum

Tape

Tape wraps around drum

HELICAL SCAN, OMEGA WRAP FORMAT

scan. The short gap when the head leaves the edge of the tape coincides with the field blanking period.

Reel-to-reel recorders are mostly used but cassette recorders are used for short, frequently used items such as commercials. On all types of machine the sound track is recorded along one edge of the tape.

Synchronisation

It is important that when a tape is replayed the head follows exactly the same path as that on the recording machine. To do this a synchronising pulse is recorded on the tape which provides information for a mechanism which controls the rotating heads.

25

Where programmes are made

Most programmes originate in a studio but in a week's viewing you are likely to see others from a variety of sources including outside broadcasts, recordings and films. Often a broadcast will contain material from all these sources. This is particularly true of current affairs programmes.

The television studio

A studio is a very large enclosed space with a strong, smooth floor on which cameras mounted on trolleys called dollies can run without any jolts that might make the picture jump. Overhead there will be a construction of girders carrying lights.

Below: *A mixture of staff, cameras and actors on a typical studio set*

Top right: *A multiple set designed so that actors can move from room to room*
Bottom right: *Some of the battery of lighting used for the set above*

There is likely to be a high gallery round the walls to give access to the lights and the control rooms, whose windows will line one wall. Leading off the studio will be scenery stores and workshops.

A studio set

When you see actors apparently moving about a room they will probably be on a set. This will be an area of a studio enclosed by scenery. Several cameras will be positioned around it. One may resemble a mobile crane with a camera and its operator sitting on the end of the jib. This can be raised to provide a bird's-eye view if required. Microphones will be suspended above the set or on mobile booms. These have to be positioned so that they are out of camera shot. It is important, too, that they do not cast a shadow on the set.

The control rooms

A studio's operations are monitored and controlled from three control rooms: production control, sound control and vision control.

Crowded conditions on the set of the 'Old Grey Whistle Test' with special effects in the background

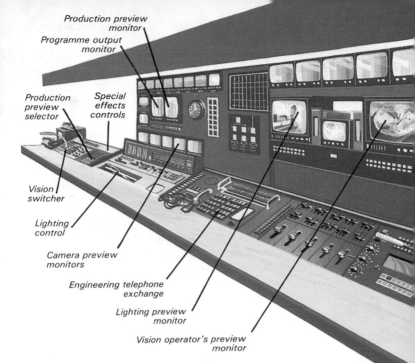

Production preview monitor

Programme output monitor

Production preview selector

Special effects controls

Vision switcher

Lighting control

Camera preview monitors

Engineering telephone exchange

Lighting preview monitor

Vision operator's preview monitor

Production control

Here the director, the production assistant, vision mixer and technical supervisor work as a team, following a prearranged plan. It is they who decide which camera's output you will be watching from moment to moment. They will be in continuous touch with those in the other control rooms and on the studio floor.

They sit at an elaborate control desk facing a bank of television screens, called monitors, linked by cable to each of the cameras and to the vision mixer. The vision mixer can switch from camera to camera in a variety of ways or combine the signals from two of them. It can feed in the output from video recorders and the telecine. Another monitor shows the signal being transmitted.

Sound control

Here the sound supervisor and the grams/tape operator work. The sound supervisor's desk will have controls for all the sources of sound; the microphones, tape recorders and record players. He will ensure that the grams/tape operator switches his apparatus in and out according to the production instructions. He will monitor the sound being transmitted or recorded and make any adjustments needed to the quality and volume.

Vision control

This team is larger. There is the vision control operator who monitors and controls the technical quality of the video signals. Then there are staff to control lighting and all those other things which make up the visual impact on you, the viewer. These include the lighting director and his assistant, a designer supervisor, who controls scenery and props, and supervisors of costume and make-up. All these directing staff have technicians operating in and around the studio below.

On the studio floor

A floor manager, four or five camera operators and staff concerned with scenery, props, wardrobe and make-up have to ensure that everything is ready in the right place as actors move from set to set.

Newscasters with supporting studio staff

Electronic News Gathering (ENG) on-the-spot news reporting

Grouped near the studio are workshops manned by technicians. They must ensure that microphones and other apparatus are in good condition and that scenery and properties are ready to be moved onto the sets when required.

The news studio

In addition to the main studios with their rapidly changing sets, there may be a smaller studio permanently equipped for news and current affairs broadcasts. Fixed microphones and monitors where input from outside sources can be watched by the presenters and newsreaders are familiar to most viewers. Then there are the telephone links into which 'hot' news may come at any time.

Teleprompter – the 12 inch on-camera script display unit fitted to the front of a television camera which allows the newsreader to read the news directly off the screen of the teleprompter and appear to be looking directly into the television camera

Teleprompter fitted onto the front of a camera

The Treasury say there's firm evidence the economy has reached

A free standing teleprompter

Outside broadcasts

Although most programmes come from the studios in the television centres, many come from permanent or temporary installations around the country and, sometimes, live from far distant parts of the world.

Permanent installations

These are to be found in famous theatres and concert halls where there are frequent broadcasts, places of special interest such as Cape Kennedy, football grounds, etc., and, very familiar, the London Weather Centre.

Outdoor events

Sporting events and demonstrations where there is often advance warning are covered by a television van linked to strategically placed cameras and commentators. Cameras will be placed to show both good general and close-up views of the action. The van will either employ a landline connection or use microwave transmission to the nearest network transmitter and on to the television centre for transmission.

Outside Broadcast coverage of a sports event

Set-piece events

These are situations where there is plenty
of time for the installation of lighting,
microphones and camera placements – these are
connected by cable to a mobile control room. This vehicle
will send the programme to the nearest network transmitter.
If transmission is not possible, landline links are set up via
special British Telecom links reserved for the use of
broadcasting authorities. Typical of this type of outside
broadcast are royal events, political conferences and
theatre performances.

Above: *Camera positions for special events must be discreetly sited*
Left: *Control vans and commentator positions*

33

News gathering

Until quite recently television reporters made films of news events and then had to get the film to a base where it could be processed and converted by telecine to television signals. That was before the coming of ENG (electronic news gathering). A reporter equipped for ENG will carry a colour TV camera with built-in amplifier and encoder. It will be slightly smaller and only a little heavier than a portable 16 mm film camera.

Around his waist he will have a battery belt carrying a number of rechargeable batteries. Also, either attached to the camera or carried by an assistant will be a videotape recorder. This recorder will be a helical scan machine using either 12 mm or 18 mm tape.

By the time this book is published, even the three tube portable camera may be out of date. A remarkable new camera has just become available. This has a single tube which can scan all three primary colours and it has a built-in recorder.

Getting the news back to base

In America the ENG reporter and his assistant are likely to carry a microwave transmitter. These transmitters can only send their very high frequency signal in a straight line, so they must be in direct line-of-sight with a receiving aerial and not too far away. Usually the reporter will work within range of a light TV van which will have an aerial to receive his signals and a powerful transmitter to get the news back to the TV centre.

In Great Britain there are very few microwave frequencies available so that sort of ENG is still experimental, except in London. In the meantime the ENG reporter either has to get his videocassettes back to the centre or send the information they contain by landline.

INSIDE A MOBILE UNIT

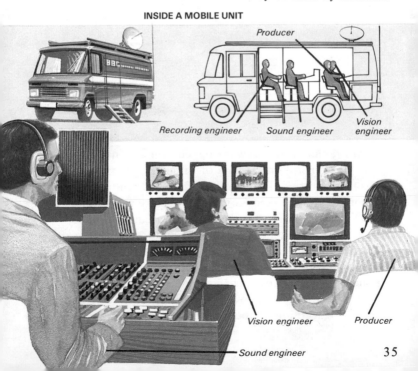

Producer

Recording engineer   Sound engineer   Vision engineer

Vision engineer   Producer

Sound engineer

35

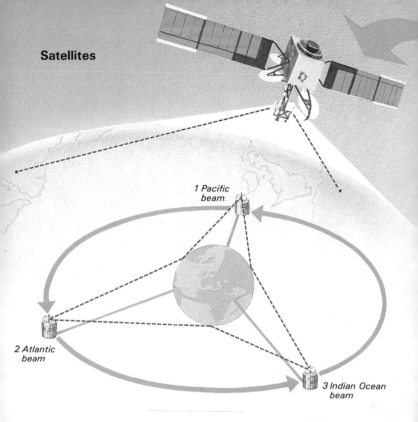

1 Pacific beam

2 Atlantic beam

3 Indian Ocean beam

At present British viewers depend on the Intelsat satellites for instant viewing of important happenings in distant countries. They are launched and controlled by an organisation called Comsat. These are synchronous satellites; that is to say, they orbit the Equator at a height of 22 300 miles (36 000 km) and travel in the same direction as the earth revolves. Their speed is matched to that of the earth's spin so that they remain at the same point above the earth's surface. There are three Intelsats in orbit and they can cover most of the earth's surface with the exception of the near-polar regions.

1 Pacific beam

An Intelsat above the Atlantic Ocean can direct a spot beam onto North America and Europe

The three Intelsats in permanent position orbiting the Equator can cover most of the world's surface with the exception of the near polar regions

2 Atlantic beam

3 Indian Ocean beam

Countries directly beneath the satellites get the best reception from them because there the signals have the least atmosphere to pass through. The further north or south from the Equator the more oblique is the angle of the satellite's beam to the earth's surface, the more atmosphere it has to pass through and the signal is therefore weaker. You can observe a similar effect when the sun is low on the horizon. It appears larger but much less bright because the atmosphere diffuses and weakens the sun's rays.

Satellite beams

The latest Intelsats have not only a global beam but hemisphere, zonal and steerable spot beams. The latter can be directed to give an extra strong signal to an area where the satellite's services are most heavily used.

An Intelsat not only provides relay facilities for television signals, but two-way telephone services as well. For example, Intelsat V which was established in orbit in 1979 has about 12 000 telephone channels. For television it has 27 transponders. A transponder receives and retransmits television signals when triggered by a special signal. Intelsat V's transponders can provide between 40 and 50 simultaneous television channels. It has a global beam, two hemisphere beams, two zonal beams and two steerable spot beams. All this is powered by solar batteries producing 12 000 watts.

Satellites retransmit using FM (frequency modulation) because this requires less power. They use a very high frequency, around 12 000 000 000 cycles per second.

Receiving satellite signals

In most countries, including Britain, satellite signals are, at present, received by large parabolic (dish-shaped) aerials. After conversion to AM these signals are rebroadcast on the country's own network.

In the USA, though, more and more 'domestic' receivers serving businesses and private homes are being installed. These use much smaller parabolic aerials, down to a mere 0.6 m diameter for a single household.

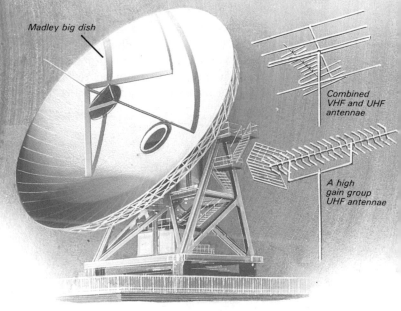

Madley big dish

Combined VHF and UHF antennae

A high gain group UHF antennae

European communications satellite (ECS)

Very soon we in Europe will have our own communications satellite launched by the European Ariane rocket. Then we, too, will begin to develop domestic receivers. It will also be much easier for ENG reporters to get their news back to the centre since their signals will be beamed up directly to the ECS and retransmitted to the centre.

Special effects

Not everything one sees on television is as real as it seems. Often a clever illusion is being created by a wide range of special effects. Most of these have been evolved by the television industry, but a few were inherited from film studios – back projection for example.

Back projection

Using this, it is possible for actors on a studio set to appear to be outdoors or driving through a city street. At the back of the set is a large rear-projection cinema screen. A film is projected onto this from the rear.

To the viewer it looks like the real thing.

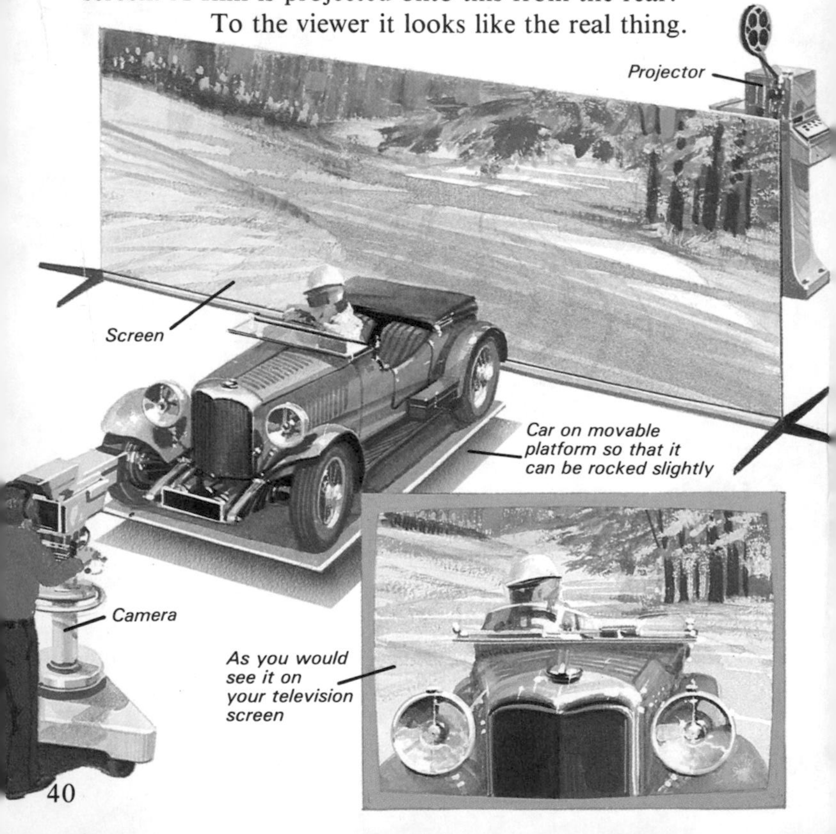

Projector

Screen

Car on movable platform so that it can be rocked slightly

Camera

As you would see it on your television screen

1 The bright blue window behind the newsreader

2 The shot to be inserted into the news story

3 The blue element is filtered out and the picture from the second source is inserted in its place

Colour separation overlay

CSO, as it is known, is a way of superimposing one picture upon another. It is an electronic method, using a device called a chroma key. You will have seen a rather bright blue 'window' or background behind a newsreader. Suddenly, the window or background is filled with a television picture of somewhere outside. The bright blue element in the original picture is filtered out and the picture from the second source put in its place.

Wipes and vision mixing

The vision mixer has at his disposal a wide range of devices for combining pictures from different cameras, tapes and telecine and also for switching from one to another. These devices are known as 'wipes'. For instance, pictures from two cameras can appear side by side on your screen without your being able to see the join. That is how you sometimes see an impersonator in one costume sitting beside himself made up for a different role and having an argument. First he did one character's part and that was tape-recorded. Then he did the other part and the two scenes combined appeared as if they were happening simultaneously.

Using wipes, pictures can be fitted into a corner of the screen or in a circle or lozenge shape or a number of other shapes. Sometimes an inserted picture may appear misty at the edges. You may have seen this effect when a close-up of a musician's hands were superimposed on a complete picture of him playing.

Digital production effects unit

This new and remarkable way of playing visual tricks is a computerised device.

With it a picture can be 'put into store' and played back within a split second in a variety of ways. The DPEU is at work when you see the screen filled with many 'copies' of the same image, like a disco dancer or a singer's head, or when the picture is spun round, turned upside down or generally goes mad on your screen.

Walking and talking

Have you ever wondered how it is that you can watch someone walking through a busy street from quite a good distance and hear him talking with not a microphone or camera in sight? Have you noticed, too, that the passers-by seem quite unaware that their fellow pedestrian is 'on the telly'?

There is a camera, of course, but it can be up to 50 feet away. The cameraman will be using a powerful narrow angle lens. As for the sound, that is coming from a tiny 'personal' microphone clipped to the speaker's clothing and linked to a radio transmitter in a pocket. Its signal will be picked up by the van's aerial.

The frontiers and beyond

There have been so many innovations in the last few years it is difficult to keep up to date with what is already possible, let alone forecast what will happen in the next decade. However, the following are a few areas of present and future change.

Home video

There are several systems for recording programmes from your receiver and replaying them at leisure. Also pre-recorded films and other programmes can be bought. Videodiscs are now available. They are similar in size to the discs you play on your record player, but work on a different principle.

Teletext

There are now three organisations providing information for the viewer to see on his TV screen by pressing a few keys on a separate piece of equipment. The BBC provides CEEFAX, the IBA offers ORACLE and PRESTEL comes from British Telecom. The latter, however, is a telephone service linked to the TV set not by broadcast methods as in the other two. In them, the teletext signals are slotted into the field blanking periods.

TV games

You may be one of those who already have a device in your home to enable you to play all sorts of games on your television. If you have, you are using a specialised micro-computer.

44

Computers

It is now possible to buy micro-computers which can do the household and business accounts and store a mass of useful information. They use the TV screen for display. You may have used such a system in your school.

Cable television

Several companies send TV signals by coaxial cable into the homes of people who cannot get a good signal through an ordinary aerial. This often happens in blocks of flats and among tall city buildings which block the radio waves.

At present this is a rather expensive system but a new type of multi-channel cable made of many hair-thin fibres of very pure glass will begin to be laid throughout Britain. This will be much cheaper and more efficient.

Flat TV sets and large screens

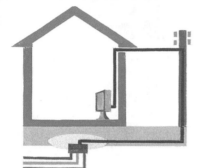

Scientists are working hard to produce a TV set thin enough to hang on the wall like a picture. At present the electron gun protrudes from the back of the set. One solution might be to fit it sideways and bend the electron beam. Others may involve getting rid of the gun altogether. Large screens are still rather unsatisfactory but an efficient one for colour TV is sure to become widely available before very long. Combine these two inventions and the result might be wall-to-wall TV.

Extra technical information

The information which follows is for readers who want to go a little more deeply into the subject. If you are interested in going even further, perhaps with a view to becoming an engineer or technician at a television studio, you will find on page 51 some careers information.

Amplifiers

These are devices to increase electrical output. Usually these are transistors or FETs (field effect transistors).

Anode

An electrode with a positive charge, i.e., electrons in an electric current flow towards it. Thus it is the path by which electricity enters a battery, valve or cathode ray tube.

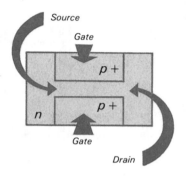

A FIELD EFFECT TRANSISTOR

Cathode

An electrode with a negative charge, i.e., the electrons of an electric current flow from it. It is the path by which electricity leaves a battery or valve.

Cathode rays

A stream of electrons coming from a thermionic cathode in a vacuum tube.

Deflection coils

Electromagnetic coils around the perimeter of a cathode ray tube. One coil is used to deflect the beam horizontally and another to deflect it vertically. The beam is controlled so that it scans a target or screen.

Dichroic mirrors

Are used instead of or as part of a prism in a video camera or telecine. Two are usually used. They are glass plates coated with a thin film of material which reflects light of one primary colour and passes the other two. Mirror 1 – this reflects blue and passes red and green. Mirror 2 – this reflects red and passes green.

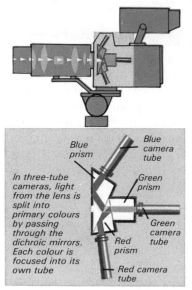

In three-tube cameras, light from the lens is split into primary colours by passing through the dichroic mirrors. Each colour is focused into its own tube

Blue prism
Blue camera tube
Green prism
Green camera tube
Red prism
Red camera tube

Electrodes

Odos is a Greek word meaning road or path, so an electrode is a path by which electricity can enter or leave a battery, cathode ray tube or valve.

Electron gun

A device used in camera tubes and television receiver display tubes to produce an electron beam. The electrons are accelerated, focused into a narrow beam and further accelerated towards a screen or target.

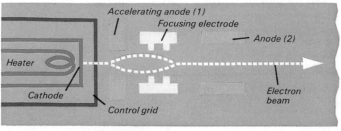

Accelerating anode (1)
Focusing electrode
Anode (2)
Heater
Cathode
Control grid
Electron beam

DIAGRAM OF AN ELECTRON GUN

Electron multiplier

An electronic tube with a cathode and a number of dynodes. A dynode is an anode which is a secondary emitter, i.e., it is made of a metal which emits extra electrons when bombarded by an electron stream. The multiplier is, in fact, an amplifier in which the electrons from the cathode multiply progressively as they pass from dynode to dynode. The more dynodes the more powerful the final current.

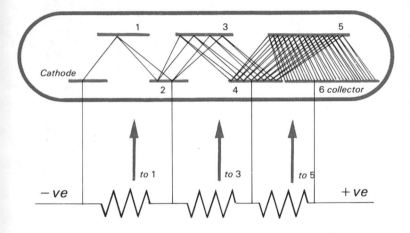

Focusing coils

Coils around the perimeter of a cathode ray tube which set up a magnetic field that causes the electrons from the cathode to converge into a beam.

Focusing electrodes

Cylindrical electrodes around the perimeter of an electron gun which set up an electrostatic field that causes the electrons from the cathode to converge into a beam.

48

Grid

An electrode consisting of either a wire mesh or a metal plate with a hole in it. The control grid in an electron gun is of the metal plate type and serves to vary the intensity of the electron stream from the cathode.

Ionosphere

A layer of the earth's upper atmosphere extending from 50 miles above the surface upwards to over 200 miles. This part of the atmosphere is ionised, i.e., composed of atoms which are electrically charged. It has the capacity to reflect some frequencies of radio waves.

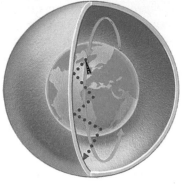

••• Shortwaves reflected.
━━ Longwave bent

Landlines

These are not ordinary telephone cables but consist of coaxial cables, a cable with an inner conducting core sheathed in insulating material and an outer layer made of woven metal which is usually earthed. Coaxial cable is not affected by external electric fields which might interfere with the very high frequency signals it is designed to carry.

TELEVISION COAXIAL CABLE

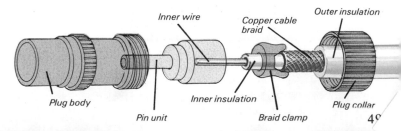

Inner wire
Copper cable braid
Outer insulation
Plug body
Pin unit
Inner insulation
Braid clamp
Plug collar

Vision mixing and wipes — a closer look

A pleasing way to remove one signal and bring in another is to fade one out and fade another in. This is done by a fader which reduces or increases the amplitude of the signal. The same device may be used to fade two signals up together.

Another way to remove a signal from the screen is to use a wipe which, appropriately, wipes the signal in one of a variety of ways. One commonly seen is the iris wipe which wipes the signal from the perimeter of the screen inwards with a reducing aperture resembling the shape of the human eye's iris as it contracts.

Some other wipes are:

Box:	expanding and collapsing rectangle
Horizontal:	an up and down wipe
Vertical:	wiping from left or right
Diagonal:	from any corner
Diamond:	expanding or collapsing

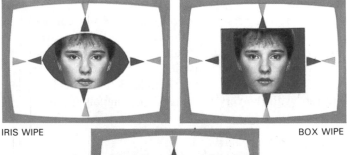

IRIS WIPE

BOX WIPE

HORIZONTAL WIPE

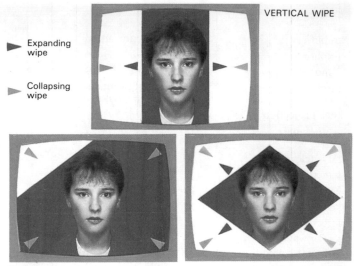

VERTICAL WIPE

Expanding wipe

Collapsing wipe

DIAGONAL WIPE

DIAMOND WIPE

A technical career in television

The BBC and IBA and other programme companies recruit between the ages of 18 and 26. One starts as a trainee assistant and needs the following qualifications: GCE O levels in at least English, mathematics and physics:

GCE A level or an equivalent technical certificate in either mathematics or physics.

You should have a full knowledge of electricity and magnetism and be able to demonstrate a strong interest and in-depth knowledge of the field in which you wish to work. For instance, if you wish to become a camera operator you will need to know about photography, stage lighting, picture composition, lenses and their uses, drama and current affairs.

Index